ROAD CORRYVRECKAN

A HISTORY USHERETTE BOOK

BY

SARAH MILLER WALTERS

Copyright © Sarah Miller Walters 2017

Cover Design by Howard Taylor

Introduction

In December 1945, Powell and Pressburger released their latest film. It was entitled 'I Know Where I'm Going' and it featured the actors Roger Livesey and Wendy Hiller. The star of the film was the wild landscape around the Scottish island of Mull. The story concerned a headstrong young woman (Hiller) who is journeying to a fictional island called Kiloran to marry a wealthy industrialist. She absolutely knows where she is going – it is towards a life of security, comfort and power. However, her crossing from the mainland is thwarted by rough weather. She is blocked from taking that final step to the life that she has planned out and she becomes increasingly agitated. Finally, she bribes a naïve young sailor to get her over to Kiloran – and they almost lose their lives in the process. The Corryvreckan whirlpool between Kiloran and the mainland almost claims them.

The near-suicidal action is prompted by the fact that she is beginning to lose control. The real Laird of Kiloran (Livesey) is on leave from the navy and is staying in the same house, awaiting calmer seas. They have a mutual attraction and Hiller's character realises that is she doesn't marry her wealthy fiancée now, she will fall for the Laird and lose all that she dreamed of. At one point they exchange the following lines:

"People around here are very poor I suppose."

"Not poor, they just haven't got money."

"It's the same thing."

"Oh no, it's something quite different."

Finally, after her near-death experience at Corryvreckan, she realises the value of this philosophy and she submits to her fate.

The following stories follow six fictional audience members at the film's 1945 release. In part one, each character watches the film with a certainty that they also know where they are going. In part two, we observe these characters as they experience their own version of Corryvreckan. Life takes them, spins them around and spits them out again in a new and unexpected direction. An epilogue lets you know how they got on afterwards.

We all have at least one Corryvreckan moment in life. Some of us have several. Let's thank Michael Powell and Emeric Pressburger for putting a name to it – and providing such startling imagery to go with it.

Part One - How Long Will The Gale Last?

On Foot, to the Devon Constabulary

It had been his intention to go straight to the police station. His first wife had been in the dining room when he first came downstairs. He hadn't been in the mood to speak to her at all, but she had barely stopped to draw breath. From the second that he sat down at the table he had suffered a barrage of questions and complaints. What was he going to do now that his release from the army was imminent? Had he given any thought whatsoever to the future? Had he noticed that the children needed new shoes? She had the coupons but where was the money? Her allowance was still the same as it had been in 1938.

He had eventually stood, drained his teacup (barely tasting the tepid liquid) and lifted his sad brown eyes.

"I will attend to matters today."

He then left the suburban villa without a backward glance. The only possessions that he took with him were the contents of his jacket pocket. He walked to the centre of Plymouth with an immediate resolve that today would be the end of it all. The game was up. Time to meet with the consequences. It wasn't fun anymore. In fact, had it ever been fun?

As he considered the dearth of cheer in his life now that the war was over, and the gloomy future that no doubt awaited him, he walked past a cinema. At that very moment, a little chap in a faded uniform was throwing open the doors. The aroma of bodies and stale smoke crept onto the pavement. It reminded him of barracks and comradeship. Just a quarter of a mile from his intended destination, he deviated. There was a little loose change in his pocket, might as well blow it on something enjoyable. No doubt watching the pictures was not allowed in prisons.

He was the first in. The young usherette shined her torch about the empty seats and smilingly told him to take his pick. That was the trouble, he thought. He always did just help himself. He sat at the end of the back row and, turning away from the supporting feature he looked carefully at the usherette.

"I don't think I've seen you here before…are you new?"

"I've just transferred here. I was working at the one in Torquay until last week."

"I must say, the uniform suits you tremendously well, my dear."

"Oh! Thank you. I was thinking of joining the WAAFs but now the war's finished there doesn't seem to be a lot of point does there? I like their uniform better."

"Oh yes, that is a shame, it would have suited you so well."

Within ten minutes, he had arranged to meet the usherette on the Hoe on her day off. He wasn't sure why he did this. If pressed, he might have said that he just wanted to check that he could still do it. But really, he just couldn't help himself.

The pair chatted until more people began to arrive and take seats around him. He smoked his way through the supporting features, wondering how he would phrase his confession to the police. Finally, the main film began. 'I Know Where I'm Going'. He smiled to himself. 'So do I.' he thought. This was the first time that the idea of prison began to take hold. 'I am going to prison, and my life will never recover.'

The girl in the film slept on the train and dreamed of her wedding. He would be sleeping in an equally incongruous place, reflecting on his own trips into matrimony. The girl in the film went into her marriage with purpose and strategy. Why did he lack those kinds of qualities? He had barely known what he was doing at both of his weddings. And then the date that he had just made with the usherette. Ridiculous. He was mere flotsam on the tide of human nature.

That girl in the film was really getting on his nerves. Like both of his wives did. So sure, always in search of an easy life, never content to put themselves at the mercy of their own feelings. He stood up and walked towards the exit, winking at the usherette as he passed her. Out in the extraordinarily fresh air, he took his bearings again and turned towards the police station. He would have arrived there in five minutes, but instead he found himself heading for the Hoe. It was almost lunchtime now, the low winter sun couldn't warm the wind that rushed up from the sea. Mothers pushed perambulators purposely, their thin coats and headscarves billowing about them. A young boy, the same age as his youngest, Peter, ran up and down the path making aeroplane noises. The boy met his gaze and smiled up at him. "My father's coming home today. He flies aeroplanes!" The boy stretched out his arms and circled him before being called away.

"What have I told you about speaking to strange men, child!"

He supposed that it might be possible to see Peter again one day, but how would Peter speak to him? Would he even call him father? He'd never really felt like a father to the boy, even though they were the image of one another.

He let the wind buffet him along the paths, getting closer to the edge of the land. Finally, facing the grey water, he practiced out loud what he should say when he faced the desk sergeant.

"I have come to hand myself in. I have committed bigamy."

By Car, to the Lancastria Grand Hotel

Catherine had told Simpkins to bring the car round for nine o'clock. Her appointment was for one o'clock at a hotel in central Manchester. It wouldn't take above an hour to get there, even if they went particularly slow to conserve petrol. But she couldn't hang around at home any longer than was necessary. Since she had realised her current predicament, Henry had set her nerves on edge more than ever before and breakfast time was the worst. She had deliberately arranged to be leaving the house just as he would be emerging from his bedroom. In the event, he came down the stairs as she stood in the elegantly tiled hallway, looking out for the car. She had a small suitcase at her feet.

"I'm having a couple of days away with Mollie Weston, she needs a break and some company poor thing, after what she's been through."

Catherine had already told Henry this last night. He had grunted acknowledgement from behind the latest issue of the local newspaper. But still, she had to repeat herself as the car finally pulled up.

"I should be back on Friday."

"Yes, alright. Nice if you can get the time off, I must say." Henry picked up the pile of post from the occasional table and went into the dining room.

They travelled to Manchester with the car window wound all the way down. Simpkins didn't comment, he merely pulled his coat collar up against the December chill. Catherine noted his relief when it was time for her to get out of the car, and felt a little guilty. Her aim had been to cause as little inconvenience as possible to everyone. She was the only one who should suffer.

Simpkins drove away, leaving her outside the entrance to Victoria Station. She had three hours to kill before…well, a cup of tea in the station buffet would pass some of it on. When it came to swallowing the thick, deep brown liquid however, she realised that she wasn't in the mood for it. Perhaps a walk would calm the nerves. But after 15 minutes of that she became tired. A cinema loomed. 'I Know Where I'm Going' the poster announced to the passing traffic. 'So do I.' she thought. 'Straight to hell. May as well see what this is about.'

The film intrigued Catherine from the beginning. Because she saw herself up there. She had once been determined to marry at any cost to herself. She had pursued Henry so well that he had proposed to her before he even knew where he was. She had given him two sons and had waited up faithfully after every board meeting, every town council meeting and every Freemasons dinner. She had waded through years of loneliness in order that she would never be without anything else in life. War had broken out twenty years after her wedding. She joined the WVS and realisation dawned that she had simply not lived her life how it was meant to be lived. The trouble was, Catherine's affairs of the heart had not taken such a neat turn of events as was being played out on screen. First to crack (but not open) the brittle shell that had formed around her was an army officer from Devon. They had met at a local dance, and he had used his considerable, inexplicable charm to gain toehold in her affections. He wooed her with his sad brown eyes and a willingness to discuss the poetry of Thomas Hardy. She nearly let him further into her life, but fortunately one evening she saw him leaving the cinema with Cynthia Drysdale and the penny dropped. Catherine managed to laugh at herself for being so taken in, then she pulled herself together and carried on.

Because she was used to handling cars, she was given regular driving jobs by the WVS – taking messages, people and supplies around the Lancashire and Cheshire areas. It was through her regular stops at the local garage that she first made the acquaintance of Bill Tanner. He was over a decade older than she was, he was widowed and he lived alone in an extension to his oily workshop. The rusty petrol pumps were the limit of his horizon. When he wasn't scratching his head over vehicles that needed non-existent replacement parts, he was on parade with the Home Guard. He felt the lack of feminine influence in his life, and so the women drivers that now ended up on his forecourt were welcomed. He explained things to them, never assumed or laughed at ignorance, a refreshing outlook that made him popular. His chats with Catherine became so frequent, that he began to invite her through the domestic door of his workshop for a cup of tea. Mostly, she was in too much of a hurry to accept, but having enjoyed the chat, she promised to return when she had a spare hour one day. Once that promise had been made, she felt a little obliged to keep it….but mostly she wanted to keep it. Occasional visits began to be slotted into their early evening schedules while Henry was at his interminable council meetings.

Tea and chat at Bill's newspaper-covered table turned to tea and sympathy as their histories revealed themselves. The sympathy progressed to a goodbye hug, and one day a chaste kiss on the cheek. Then, after one particularly bloody day when Catherine's youngest son had returned to school without saying goodbye, and Henry had yet again derided her WVS work, a chaste kiss progressed rather suddenly. It ended with her green WVS uniform slung across Bill's bedroom chair, his overalls entangled inside it. She returned four days later. He waited for chastisement and was ready to beg forgiveness; but she only meekly asked him if they might possibly do it again. This time, they laughed about it.

"Do you do this with every passing WVS driver?" she asked him.

"No!" he protested. "You're the only girl in green for me."

Bill Tanner's bed became a place of refuge quite regularly for the next year and a half. Both knew it could go no further and accepted their actions for what they were – a small slice of pleasure in an overwhelmingly dull life. It was to be grabbed where possible then locked away, not spoken of. Pregnancy had not occurred to either of them. They somehow viewed their little pleasure as being quite innocent – and both assumed that Catherine was too old.

But she was not too old to become pregnant, as she finally realised, one queasy and horrified Sunday morning. From her ordered life she had lunged into unplanned illegitimate pregnancy and the heavy task of concealment. This was not a problem that could be shared. Bill must not know. It would spoil everything. She consulted a Manchester doctor (after gaining his details from a friend of a friend, supposedly for a fictitious village girl). He agreed to arrange an abortion for a very high fee. It was to take place in a hotel room. Catherine had sold her late mother-in-law's ruby brooch to pay for it. As the film credits went up, it was time to check in and meet the abortionist. She left the cinema feeling like she carried a lead weight for a foetus.

By Greyhound to the Life of Riley

Arthur was one of the oldest, so they'd taken pity on him and let him out of the navy quite early on. One of the first to be demobbed. He had always said that it had been his bad luck – a bit older and they'd have put him in the Home Guard instead of a boat in the freezing North Sea. But there it was. He'd got through it, got home again. Shouldn't complain.

No, he shouldn't complain. But he still felt like doing so. He was tired. But they had made him take his old job back and be grateful that they'd saved it for him. That sort of patriotism was only to be expected from the Scottish Co-op. But still, those young lasses that had been filling in could stay on as far as he was concerned. They had the energy for it. Just being back home with the missus and the family was tiring enough. He'd got his first grandchild as the war was drawing to a close. A beautiful little girl with a grand set of lungs. The problem with this was that she was living in his house until her father got demobbed and he wasn't nearly so high on the list as Arthur had been. He thought he might finally get a good night's sleep now he was home. That had gone out of the window. And to top it all, while he and his son-in-law had been away, his wife and daughter had been listening to radio programmes and reading magazines and getting some daft ideas. Apparently, they had to make an effort to make their husbands feel a part of their lives again. Arthur's wife was now insisting that every Friday evening was "their night". He was not allowed to make any other arrangements, or to go to the pub or have an early night. He was instead under instruction that they were both to "dress up nice" and leave the house together at 7pm. Their evening would then take the following schedule: a visit to the cinema, one drink only in The Ship Inn and then a fish supper. He didn't mind the latter two so much – although more than one drink would have been welcomed – it was the visit to the cinema that got him down. Films did nothing for him. Each one was an hour and a half out of his life that he would never get back again. Then there was the depressing news and everything else to sit through. But if it kept his Mary happy… Ah well. A man's life was never his own.

One particular evening, the film was called 'I Know Where I'm Going.' Mary insisted "You'll like this one, Arthur. It's filmed in Scotland mostly. Mull I think they said."
"I've never been to Mull." He told her, and he determined even more that he wouldn't like it. Just because they'd filmed the damn thing in his own

country, didn't mean he had to enjoy it. Damn fools, women sometimes. His pink ears turned red.

Arthur sat back in his seat. He popped an aniseed ball into his pursed mouth and began to seek escape within his own head. His chosen topic of muse was entitled 'ways to make money and therefore not have to work quite so much'.

He could start making something to sell.

Too much extra work to begin with.

Find another job that was a bit easier, maybe involved sitting down.

Possible, but might not get paid so much.

Get an allotment and sell vegetables.

No.

Arthur was momentarily distracted by a handsome woman appearing on the screen. She had just walked into the house from the moors with her dogs.

Dogs.

Bob Foster.

Dogs.

Arthur and Bob Foster had been shipmates for the last two years of the war. He was a young kid – although he looked much older than his years. Life had not been kind to Bob. But whenever they had shore leave, Bob had always come back on board smiling. It was that time when they had to dock on the Manchester Ship Canal for some repairs that Arthur got to the bottom of it. They were allowed off the boat for the evening and Bob had leapt on to the quay and accosted a WVS woman in a green overcoat who was stood by her car waiting for someone. He had demanded of her urgently if there was a dog track nearby. She had looked at him blankly – hadn't a clue. The expression on her face had been a picture. But she laughed with them about it – she sounded posh but she had no airs or graces. She sent Bob and Arthur on to a pub and told them to ask there – they had told him that there was no greyhound racing to be had that night. So instead they had supped a couple of pints of ale and discussed the art of betting on the dogs. Bob told him that he had a system, that he often won a packet. He reckoned that when he got demobbed, he'd go and work the dog tracks all around the country. The secret was to stay sober, he said. Everyone else went along with a skin-full, too intent on plain enjoyment. Gambling is a serious business.

Arthur decided that he would start frequenting Powderhall dog track, try and run into Bob, get him to teach his old mate the secrets. He could then build up enough money in his post office account until he no longer needed to work. That's where Arthur was going.

By Bicycle to Gretna Green

Bernard had made the final leg of his journey home by boat. Carried back by a mainly Scottish crew, he had sailed into Leith, before going onto his hometown by two trains. While on-board ship, the salt wind had whipped the burn scars on his face raw, so he had sat mainly below, wondering what would happen next. Of course he was returning to work on his father's farm, and he would probably inherit the tenancy. But he didn't think that he had any feelings for his homeland anymore. Would he settle back down, or should he perhaps move to Newcastle and find work in the city? His reverie had been disturbed by a couple of sailors. One, a greying man with pink ears, had just received news of both his demob and the birth of his grandchild. His mate had whooped and patted him on the back but he had merely grumbled away about this and that. In the end his mate swivelled his eyes and danced his way up the ladder towards the deck laughingly calling "Ya miserable old bastard" over his shoulder.

Bernard began to think of family too, and of his divorce. It was doubtful any girl would want to marry him with these scars and that past. Perhaps he ought to do something noble. Become a doctor, dedicate himself to other burns patients like he had been. Perhaps an understanding nurse would take him on. When he got off the train at his home station, he found the north Pennine hills much as he had left them, but his mind was still changing, his thoughts scudding about like clouds over the peaks.

His father understood, he was glad to have his son back and tried to re-introduce him to the farm gently. "Get to know the land again, you've been away from her a long time." he told Bernard "Get out on your bike, go for walks. Why not join the village cycling club?"

"Is that still going?"

"Of course it is. Well, it was the land girls mainly that kept it going. They wanted to see the sights you see, all being city girls. Mrs Asher at the Butchers – she runs it, go and see her."

"I might."

"That's right. Take the time you need. If you and the land aren't friends then farming won't work for you."

One bright October day, Bernard wheeled his old cycle to the meeting point outside the village hall. He pushed off in a hap-hazard line of a dozen bikes of mainly late middle aged men and women, evangelical about the fresh air and enjoying the British countryside. The only two people close to Bernard's age were the butcher's lad and Barbara, the local solicitor's daughter. She had been a child when he had left for war but now she had become a serious young woman, dressed in brown. She believed in farming, and knew all about wildflowers and birds. Other club members held her in high esteem as she had made her own cardigan from bits of wool that she found around the sheep fields. They drifted together and pedalled at the same pace. She reminded him of all he had forgotten with her sudden enthusiasms.

By December, the club's cycle rides had become fewer and shorter, but Bernard and Barbara's own meetings had increased in frequency. It began with an extra bike ride of their very own, followed by a bus trip to Barnard Castle. Now, they sat in the back row of the cinema in the local town. They hoped that no-one they knew would see them. After their trip to Barnard Castle, Barbara's father had found out and had made some enquiries. A divorced tenant farmer. This was not what Barbara's parents had hoped for. The pair had tried to carry on meeting discreetly, avoiding walking together in the main street and not always cycling together when out with the club. But in villages of that size, nothing could remain unnoticed. Barbara's father had decided to have a talk with her. Now that war was over and she was still relatively young, perhaps she ought to have a short spell at a finishing school. Her parents decided that it was time that she broadened her horizons, saw a little more of the world…met more people. They could just about manage to afford a spell in London for her.

Barbara was quite certain that the north Pennine hills was enough of the world for her. She didn't care if she never went anywhere else. She told Bernard this very fact after marching straight across three miles of fields to his farm in a hurling rage. He gave her a drink of milk and leaned her against the 5 bar gate. "And this exact spot? How does it suit you?"
"I'm not 21 yet, father wouldn't allow it."

"I can wait."

"I should hope so." She kissed him delicately, on the burned side of his face.

And so they sat at the cinema, watching a very headstrong young woman head towards her own wedding, allowing nothing to stand in her road. The film reached the scene where she tried to cross the swirling sea in a tiny boat.

"She's determined, isn't she?" Barbara whispered.

"Yes." Bernard breathed in her ear. "It's the war, it's sent some of us that way." He squeezed her hand.

"What are you thinking?" She could tell by the way he moved his fingers that something was developing in his mind.

"Scotland. Gretna Green's in Scotland."

"So it is." She turned to look at the jagged outline of his face, not minding that the lead romantic characters on screen were possibly about to drown.

"We could cycle there!"

"We could…and we will!"

By Train to a Small Town in the Provinces

The station at Southampton Docks was packed full of humanity in all its stinking glory. This was sort of alright, Sheila had become used to uncomfortable places over the past couple of years. ENSA had despatched her to some of the most crowded cities on earth. She had delivered humorous songs to fetid halls full of men who had been disabled, blinded and burned. She had slept in dormitories beneath mosquito nets and dodged scorpions in the latrines. But the cold did for her. That December wind, that had blown them over the Solent and into the docks… She had forgotten what it was like to have finger-ends that ached without mercy. And this was the south coast, supposedly milder than home.

Sheila said goodbye to her travelling companion. Another actress, she was going home to start a domestic life, keeping house for her husband. She was on her second marriage already, her first having failed as she found her husband's facial burn injuries utterly repellent. The two women exchanged addresses, but Shelia doubted they would stay in touch. Domesticity didn't interest her.

It felt like madness to try and get on a train now. Two ships had recently berthed and another was loading up with a stream of women and young children. The noise was appalling. Perhaps if she went for a warm somewhere, came back later for a train. Maybe try and get one at the Central Station. Might be a better chance of getting a seat. Sheila and her baggage walked up into the gap-toothed town with the wind chasing behind. Finally – a place to go –a cinema with a café. First she had tea and a rock cake to remind her stomach that it was British after all. Then she slipped into the cinema, a foggy warmth of cigarette ends and woollen coats and scarves. Huddled into her seat, her finger ends and toes tingled as the blood crept back in. The main feature had just started. 'I Know Where I'm Going.'

The train on the screen – how sweet that they used a child's model – made its way up the British map. No doubt her journey would not be so quick, and she was only going half that distance. The trouble was, Sheila knew where she was going, but didn't know what would happen when she got there. She was heading home, back to where she came from. She would spend a little time with her parents, visiting the relatives, commiserating with some and celebrating with others. But then…? She had a little money to tide her over but it would only go so far. She needed to work, and that work must be in the theatre. No doubt her father would urge her into a proper job, while her mother would engineer introductions to returning servicemen. But really, she hoped that there would be another destination – Manchester or Sheffield perhaps, close enough to pop home, far enough away to be able to live in digs with other girls like her. She would have to make it her business to visit all of the repertory theatres in turn. Surely with her experience one of them would be glad to have her?

Sheila realised that she must show the same tenacity that was being demonstrated on screen by Wendy Hiller. She knew that as soon as the welcome home was over, the campaign would begin to keep her there. She too would have to be underhand, risk the whirlpool of domesticity to get to where she wanted to be. Perhaps she could pay her way into somewhere, offer to supply something that the theatre needed. Costumes? Work for free for a week or two? She must make a plan, keep it up her sleeve.

The film ended. Sheila acknowledged to herself that it wasn't just the crowds that had put her off the attempt to make the journey home. It was a reluctant curtain down on her ENSA work, her travels. But they would be waiting for her in that dead end place, she would have to go. She made her way to the Central Station and boarded a train that was ultimately bound for York.

By Boat to New York

Edie sank thankfully into the tip-up chair and placed her shopping basket at her feet. She didn't mind that the main feature was halfway through, it was the warmth and the seat that she wanted. Finally, her extremities began to make their presence felt again. Her right hand was bloodless after carrying her heavy basket along the Norwich streets. She lit a cigarette and unbuttoned her coat. Dancers jogged on the screen, a plump boy in an RAF uniform propositioned his sweetheart. Just like Robert had done to her. She smiled to herself and settled back as she realised that the film was set in Scotland.

US Airman Robert McBride wasn't Scottish himself. He was a grocer's son from New York. But one of the first things that he had told her was that his grandparents came from the Highlands, and that he was determined to spend his first leave travelling up there. But if she didn't mind waiting, his next leave would be all hers. She did mind waiting as a matter of fact, but to tell him so would have been a grave error. Edie's friend, Doris Foster, had tutored her in the art of ensnaring a Yankee serviceman.

"Don't let on that you're keen. Don't get all pushy and ask questions about everything. Just smile and oblige."

They had met at a couple of dances before he did his whistlestop tour of his ancestral land; where she managed to oblige him just enough to keep him interested and maintain her honour at the same time. She had even ducked out of work to wave him off on his journey from the railway station, accidentally-on-purpose giving him a glimpse of her stocking top as she fetched out a hanky to wave with. Doris Foster had been enormously impressed with Edie's conduct, and had taken much of the credit when Edie and Robert became engaged.

They had married fairly quickly – "Who knows if my next leave will be my last, honey!" Edie entered matrimony as if she had merely won first prize in a beauty contest at Butlin's. Robert's compatriots were dropping out of the sky every week. He was her prize, one that they all thought would soon fade away into a treasured youthful memory. Their wedding photo stood on her mother's mantelpiece next to a souvenir of London.

That Robert lived to see the end of the war came as quite a surprise to everyone concerned. What would happen next was a question that got picked over like the carcass of the occasional chicken that ended up in their oven.

"Are you sure that he won't stay here?" Edie's mother asked her. "I don't see how you're going to cope in a place like New York. You get overwrought when the beach fills up at Yarmouth."

"Ma, he doesn't want to stay here. All his family are over there."

"And all your family's here!"

"But America's a better place to bring up children. They have heating and all sorts of food where Robert comes from."

"Who says there's going to be children? Your system might not cope with somewhere foreign."

"I think there already is, Ma…"

The baby had been born in November – just five weeks ago. Edie's mother had cried as she held her grandchild for the first time.

"I shan't ever see you grow up, little man." She whispered into his pale velvet ear.

Robert had already gone home and had made arrangements for his wife and child to join him. They were to sail from Southampton in a boat full of GI brides, fleeing the cold and the dark of England, never to look back. He had written:

'I can't wait to have you here and everyone is keen to meet you both. Once junior is a little bit bigger, we could really use your help in the store too – business is good. So you make sure you get a good rest on the boat!'

Edie had read the letter while laid in bed. Her mother did a nappy change while a stew simmered on the stove. There was nothing more to do than have a good cry. She had then got up, readied herself and gone into town to buy a few supplies for the journey before ending up in the cinema, watching 'I Know Where I'm Going.'

Edie's mother insisted on travelling with her and the baby as far as Southampton. She would see the boat leave, be with them both until the final possible moment. And anyway, surely Edie would need help on the train, battling through London to get to Waterloo. It wasn't a journey for someone as delicate as her.

*****

Part Two – As Long As The Wind Blows

Still On Foot, Heading For the Devon Constabulary

He stood on the grass and looked out into Plymouth Sound. The water was a grey moving mass, the occasional white wave broke on the surface. A Thomas Hardy poem came to mind, and he began to repeat the opening line to himself:

"We stood by a pond that winter day."

Except, by necessity, he could only stand there singularly in case he was seen by one or the other of his faded loves. Despite having two families, to be a "we" was practically impossible for him.

His reverie was broken by the rumbling of wheels behind him, moving along at a leisured pace. A child was being scolded by an old and tired voice as they walked past.

"Boys that keep on being naughty like that often grow up to be dead. Or even worse – in prison! Wait till I tell your parents about this disobedience."

He turned around and followed them off the Hoe – a Nanny with a heavy hooded perambulator and a small slouching boy being dragged by the wrist. He made for the police station again. By the time he arrived he was light headed. He supposed that it was due to lack of food. Would they feed him in the cells? He stood outside the dour public entrance.

"We stood by a pond that winter day."

"Boys that keep on being naughty grow up to be dead...or worse – in prison."

A constable approached him.

"Everything alright, Sir?"

He whipped around to look at the uniform. It was filled by a friendly faced Bobby, who probably thought that he was just an ordinary gentleman wanting to report a petty theft.

"Yes. Quite alright. I was going in but I've changed my mind. You chaps have enough to do."

He turned on his heel and walked away briskly, before the constable could protest. He walked on through town, wherever the wind pushed him. Eventually, he caught sight of Brunel's railway bridge over the Tamar, which he stopped to contemplate from a street corner while lighting his last cigarette. One could stand on the parapet of the open section before the metalwork began, and simply dive off into oblivion. Nannies were always right. Prison was worse than death. So that is what he would do.

He walked towards the railway, eventually finding his way onto the track a little distance away from the bridge. The great grey tubular mouth drew him onwards. He walked rhythmically along the sleepers…
"We stood by a pond that winter day…" each word a step forward.
Grey vapour began to emanate from the bridge, little wisps at first, and then a rising cloud. He saw the black dial of the engine smokebox progressing around the curve – the track was singled so he pushed himself into the edge. But the train crew had observed him. The brakes were applied and as the engine cab slipped away past him, the driver called out.

The train sighed its way to a final halt. The fireman jumped down from the cab and began to walk back to where he had cowered untouched – but only just.

Seeing the heavily built and overalled man approaching, he turned and ran along the ballast edge towards the bridge parapet. Twisting to look over his shoulder, he saw that the fireman was gaining on him. Curious heads began to bob out of the carriage windows. He scrambled up the brickwork and made a feeble diving pose. Voices called out, doors clicked open and ballast slushed. He was just wondering whether to bother holding his nose when he was violently tugged from behind. He landed on his back, prostrate.

"Help me lift him into the carriage. I'm a doctor. I'll look after him until we get into the station."

This gruff, educated voice spoke over him, he felt his arms and legs pinned by two sets of hands. A small ripple of applause accompanied his inelegant entry into the train.

"We'll fetch a copper off the station when we've stopped. Keep him in the carriage until then." The fireman left these instructions before he made his way back to the engine. The journey towards the Devon constabulary was finally back on course. The doctor spoke to him, tried to find out his troubles, but he would not respond. As they edged into Plymouth station, the doctor took his arm, it was rather too-tight a grip which irritated him. He pulled his arm from the doctor's grasp, found himself up against the carriage door. The window was still down – it was the work of instinct to open the door and try to escape. The train was moving slowly enough, he reckoned he could run across the track and get lost in the sidings. He would not be handed over like a criminal.

He jumped. The Cornish Express was just moving off south on the adjacent track. The two met, head on.

At the Lancastria Grand Hotel

Catherine checked into the Lancastria, although the hotel was not nearly as grand as the name claimed. It certainly made an effort to appear so. Potted palms hid the threadbare bits in the carpet; the gilding on the cornicing had been touched up. She was given the key to her room by an old man who had cut himself while shaving. She felt him watching her as she took the stairs up to a room on the first floor. The soft furnishings were worn but the bed linen was clean. A railway line passed by within a few feet of the window. It was raised up to her first floor level, and she could see the faces of the train crews as they trundled by in their leaky engines. She went to open the window a little, so that some air could at least circulate, no matter how grimy. The driver of a passing goods train turned and caught her eye. He reminded her instantly of Bill. She half closed the curtains and sat down to wait. It was no good trying to read anything, trying to think or to plan. Her head would only contemplate what was about to take place in this dark little room. She flitted about from feelings of shame to desperation for the man to arrive so that it would all be over. Apparently he was in demand, she was warned that he might be a little late. Procedures didn't always go to plan.

Catherine stood and went to the door. She was thirsty, a cup of weak tea would be appreciated. Or perhaps she should have a gin. There was no-one in the corridor outside, no footsteps approached. She checked her watch, it was twenty minutes to two. If she went downstairs she might miss him when he arrived. She closed the door again and dithered about a little – looking out of the window, arranging the pillows on the bed. Footsteps approached at last…then continued on past her door. Eventually, her watch passed two o'clock. She picked up her handbag and left the room.

The same old man sat at the front desk, reading a newspaper in shirt sleeves.

"Help you, madam?"

"I'm rather in need of a cup of tea…"

"Ah, that we can provide, madam. Pop through to the lounge and Betty will attend to you."

"I see. Good. Now. I am expecting someone to call on me. If anyone asks, would you be good enough to direct them to the lounge?

"Certainly Mrs…" He frowned as he looked at the guest book, which she had deliberately signed in a rather haphazard fashion.

"Hargreaves."

"Hargreaves. Will do."

She took a seat by the door in the dark, red lined lounge. Her tea arrived promptly, but that was all. By a quarter to three, the remaining dregs of her tea were cold. She had looked at, though not read, every page of yesterday's evening news. Trains had chugged by continually. She wondered if perhaps she ought to have travelled to London, they were probably more reliable down there. If he had arrived at one o'clock, the time arranged, it would have been done by now.

There was a shuffling in the doorway. The old man from the reception desk stood there, wrestling the broad sheets of the latest newspaper. He limped towards her, folding this way, then that, until the paper became the size of a novel.

"Still waiting for your visitor, madam?" He didn't pause for her to answer the question. "Have a look at this newspaper, I've finished with it now."

He placed it onto the coffee table directly in front of her and left the room, adding over his shoulder "Just ring for Betty at the hatch if you need more tea."

Catherine watched him leave. His behaviour…it wasn't quite…something was amiss. She looked down at the newspaper that had been placed so deliberately in front of her. One story took up the central column, it was headed

Woman Found Dead in Bury Hotel

Two Men Arrested

She read on, a deep pink colour creeping up her face, heat rising from her tightly swelled stomach. The unfortunate woman had, it was reported, bled to death in a bed and been found by a chamber maid. One man had been arrested on Bury railway station in connection with the death. Another, a doctor, had been arrested at his house in Manchester later that same day. Catherine recognised the address.

Rather than panic, her initial reaction was realisation that the old man on reception had purposely given her this news report. He knew why she was here. She supposed that this hotel was one of the abortionist's regulars. Shame that she had been recognised as a woman who had surrendered to her more base instincts flooded her body and sank to her belly. She stood and made straight for the main exit from the hotel.

"I'm just going out for air. If anyone asks for me, I'll be back shortly." She called over her shoulder, unable to look reception full in the face. She ran along the main street before blindly turning into an alley, where she vomited violently into the gutter. Long after there was anything left to bring back up, she leaned against the cold bricks and wretched out dry sobs. An old woman staggered past the end of the alley, stopping to exchange her heavy shopping bag from the left hand to the right. She saw Catherine and cocked her head to one side.

"Are you alright Missis? You look awful rough."

Catherine nodded. "Thank you. I'll be fine in a moment."

"You sure you don't want me to fetch anyone?"

"Yes. There's no-one to fetch anyway."

The woman put her shopping down on the pavement corner.

"I don't like to leave you."

"No, it's alright. I'm staying at the hotel further along the road. I'll go back there and sit down."

"I should telephone someone from there, tell them to fetch you home."

"Yes I will. Thank you."

The woman picked up her bag and moved on. Catherine thought for a moment, then returned to the hotel and went into the telephone booth in the corner of the lobby. She counted out some coins, picked up the heavy receiver and asked to be put through to Tanner's Garage in her home town. There was a small mirror on the wall. She looked at herself as the line burred. It wasn't pretty.

Bill's voice came over the line, business-like, cautious.

"Bill? It's me. I'm in Manchester. I'm in a spot of trouble...can you come to me?"

"Katie? What are you doing there? Of course I'll come, where are you?"

"It's the Grand Lancastria Hotel. I've got a room here, just ask for Mrs Hargreaves at reception."

"Hargreaves?"

"Yes. I'll tell them that you're my husband, so remember that."

"Right...." His tone changed a little, "I'll be there. Sit tight old girl."

By the time Bill arrived it was just past dusk. Catherine sat in the room in darkness. Light hurt her eyes. The curtains were open and sporadic flashes illuminated the carpet as the trains slid past. She may have dozed a couple of times but she was awake as Bill tentatively knocked at the door. She called out for him to come in. He pushed open the door carefully and put his head around first.

"Found you at last!" He clicked the light switch and Catherine covered her eyes. "Sorry, startled you." He stood, unsure what was expected of him.

"Just put the lamp on by the bed…my eyes and my head…"

He did as he was bid, and then perched on the end of the bed and looked at her. "What's the trouble, Katie?"

Catherine wished that she had thought about what she had to say, rehearsed it. She could merely gasp out a sob.

"What's wrong? I'll do all I can for you. Don't worry."

"I came here to meet a man, to have it taken away but he never came he's been arrested for murder and now I don't know where to go and people are just going to know soon." Her shoulders heaved. Bill was silent. She looked up at him. "I'm sorry, I'm not making any sense I'm in such a panic."

"You came here to meet a man?"

"Yes. An abortionist Bill, I need an abortion."

"Abortion."

"Yes."

"Whose?...I mean, your husband...?"

"Bill, I told you. It's been years. I have to do something soon or Henry will notice and throw me out. I don't know what else to do. It took me long enough to sort out today, I'm at least four months on. But the man didn't come and I saw in the paper that one of his patients died and he's been arrested because of it."

"So this is my child?"

Catherine stood and went to the window. "How many mechanics do you think I've been sleeping with?"

"Right. Sorry."

They lapsed into silence. A train passed by, heavy and slow with full carriages. Passengers chatted, read, leaned back with their eyes closed. Darkness returned as the train moved on. She now saw Bill's lamp lit reflection in the window again. He perched on the bed, his elbows on his knees, hands covering his face.

"I always wanted a child. We never had any. I suppose she was never that well. That's what killed her, cancer, down there. And now it's happening and you're saying it's got to be stopped."

"I don't know any other way, Bill. Think what I would have to go through to have it. Henry would never let me see my boys again." She began to cry "I have to choose between my children. And I have to choose what I already have."

Bill stood. "Leave him anyway. Everyone's getting divorces these days, it's not so shocking. Divorce him, marry me Katie and we'll have this baby."

"I don't know, Bill."

"Henry doesn't care about you. You've said so! You deserve someone who does. Your boys are nearly grown, they can make their own minds up."

"Make their own minds up about a mother who got herself pregnant by another man and left their father. Boys like their mothers to be pure."

They lapsed into silence again. Eventually, they lay down on the bed together and passed the night on wide awake. Talking.

Still Seeking The Life of Riley

Arthur's strategy began by simply watching and noting. He made his way to Powderhall dog track one evening each week with a tiny Woolworth's notepad in his inside pocket. He watched the greyhounds circuit, and noted down each dog's number in order as the results were given out. He tracked the outcome of the favourites and even tried his hand at plotting a graph.

"Keep sober, use your head."

He remembered Bob telling him. Not a farthing was handed over to a bookmaker for three weeks. But during this time he saved bits and pieces of change in an Oxo tin that he had hidden in the hall cupboard. And he saved himself for Bob, looking out for him at every meeting, hoping that his old shipmates would be given shore leave soon.

Bob did turn up eventually, not long into the new year. Arthur was just contemplating risking a few pence on every other favourite to see how this strategy fared. Arthur first glimpsed Bob as he was handing over some paper money to a man who was flanked by a couple of toughs. He made his way over and the two old comrades greeted each other with cordial warmth. They exchanged the basic information about each other's lives until Arthur felt that he could ask the question that was bouncing around his head.

"So then Bobby lad, what trap are you betting on in the next one?"

"Me? Nah, not decided. Giving the first couple of races a miss while I check the variables."

"Oh? I thought I just saw you handing over some cash?"

"Oh that? They weren't bookies. I was just paying back what I owe some fellers. I keep my slate clean, Arthur."

"So you mean you lost some cash last time?"

"Aye, I had one of those runs of bad luck. You get them from time to time."

"I thought you had a fool-proof system? I was going to ask you to let me in on the secret."

"Oh that's right…but these systems you see, they only last for so long. Then they stop working see, and you have to take a step back and think up a new one."

"So you're just thinking up your next system tonight?"

"To begin with, aye. First couple of races, we'll watch and learn, see?"

"Righto."

The men found a position from where they could watch the racing clearly. Bob insisted on being near the track that led in from the kennels. He wanted to inspect the greyhounds as they got their first sniff of the stadium. They stood back and watched the first three races without moving. Bob wouldn't allow speaking as the dogs came out and the race went on. They stood, hands in pockets, faces muffled against a biting breeze, taking it all in. After the dogs had been led off from the third race, Bob turned to Albert. "What's that you said about betting on every other favourite? Would've worked if you'd started on the second race."

"Yes." Arthur chewed his lip. "Though if we'd started on the first race then we'd have lost both times."

"Aye but let's start now. Come on. A shilling. Next favourite."

Arthur hesitated; he had been exaggerating when he had mentioned twelve whole pennies earlier, as he explained his idea. He hadn't wanted to appear such a novice. It was more or less all he had with him.

"Come on Arthur! You'll never make anything if you hold back. And go with your instinct. Your instinct said every other favourite."

"Alright, let's put the money on." Arthur followed Bob to one of the bookmakers. He handed over his shilling and received his little slip of paper confirming his choice. They moved back to their original position and watched the dogs being led around the track.

"There she is." Bob pointed at dog number three as it trotted past them, bright eyed and sleek. A religious silence enclosed both men as their chosen hound was put into the trap. The electric hare bobbed into life and began to zip around the track. With a crack the dogs followed at a gallop. Number three was in second place until the final half, then either it powered forward or the nearest rival fell back. It was difficult to tell at such speeds. Number three, the favourite, took the race. The men soon collected their money – their shilling was returned along with a few pence. The odds had not been high.

"So we sit this race out, then back the favourite in the next one." Bob had taken Arthur's plan and made it his own. Resisting the temptation of a drink while they waited – 'you need to keep sober, keep your head.' They stood at the back of the stand this time, keeping out of it all. The favourite dog came second and Bob congratulated himself on a plan that was working.

"A shilling and two pence this time, Arthur. Keep pushing your stake up, little by little."

"The odds are a bit higher this time Bob. I don't think we stand as good a chance of winning."

"Maybe not. But if we do, well! More to play with next time!"

"I don't know. I think I'll stop at a shilling."

"Suit yourself. But that's not how you make your money. When you're on a roll, you got to go with it, see?"

"We've only had one winner!"

"Two if you count the one we didn't bet on first off."

"How much to you usually put on, Bob?

"Me? I start on a quid most times. I'm just playing at it with you, Arthur boy! Testing out your system for you."

The men gambled on three more races, winning two and losing one. They left the stadium cheerily, nipping into a pub just before last orders for a celebratory whisky. Arthur, a few pence richer, thought that he would do this again. Make a regular thing of it. Get braver as time went on and win more money. His Oxo tin would lead to something more substantial in time, he was sure of it. They left the pub as the bell rung for last orders, then head towards their own districts of the city. The streets were busy, shiny pavements reflected overcoats and boots among the gas lamp glow. The men parted ways, but before their moved off, Arthur wrote his address on the back of a scrap of paper and handed it to Bob.

"Look me up when you're next on leave. Drop by for a drink."

Bob looked over his shoulder, distracted for a moment by a movement further along the street.

Then he accepted the slip of paper.

"Righto! Cheerio!" Then he was gone.

Arthur shrugged his way home, back to his usual life.

It was four days later when Arthur heard from Bob again. An old woman in a thin coat and a headscarf knocked on the door just as Mary was clearing away the plates from their evening meal. Arthur answered the feeble rapping and was politely asked if he was Arthur who used to be in the navy. When he agreed that this description suited him, she showed him the slip of paper that he had given Bob.

"My nephew says that you gave him this…can I have a little talk with you about him?"

He opened the door wide and showed her into the kitchen. Mary looked her over and immediately sat her by the fire and offered her sandwiches and tea. "She just looked so tired." Mary explained to Arthur afterwards.

"So you're young Robert's auntie then?" Arthur opened the conversation.

"Yes, I'm his poor mother's sister. Me and the lad have only got each other now. So when he was took in hospital they fetched me.

"Hospital? What happened?" Mary stopped fussing about with the crockery and sat with the pair.

"He was roughed up the night before he was due back on ship. Some men pounced on him, kicked him about then slashed him with a knife."

"What was it about?" Mary asked, Arthur had a feeling that he didn't need to ask anything.

"Money, I suppose. I haven't asked him but he's always had trouble with debts. He just can't help himself with the gambling you see. Always thinks he's one race away from a fortune."

"I see."

"Anyway, he was asking for Arthur. I asked him who Arthur was and he gave me this bit of paper with your address on. Would you mind visiting him one evening? If it's no trouble, of course. I can tell you're a busy man." Arthur's grand-daughter had just woken.

"No trouble at all…" Arthur looked up at the ceiling. "I'll go tomorrow."

Arthur went to the hospital and found Bob with a Technicolor face.

"You look bonny."

"I feel it."

"What's it all about?"

"Just a bit of money I owed. I was late paying it back. So I had to pay another way – on account. They'll be back for more."

"Best thing you can do is get on that ship and not come back, I'd say."

"Well I wanted to ask you to help me out with getting the cash I need. Are you going to Powderhall again soon?"

"I was thinking of doing. But I don't really know."

"I was going to ask you to stick to that system. It's a good one. And put one on for me each time. You can keep the first stake out of my winnings."

Arthur looked back at the lad, and then leaned back in his chair. "I said I was thinking about it. But I've just made up my mind not to. I used to think that you were so cheerful whenever you got back on board ship because you'd won a packet. But really you were just pleased to have got there in one piece hadn't you?"

Bob closed his eyes. "I'm tired now Arthur. Perhaps you'd best leave it then."

"Yes lad, I'd best leave it. Think about what I said about leaving here and not coming back. Goodnight."

On Their Way to Gretna Green

Bernard and Barbara met, as agreed, outside the village shop. It was six o'clock in the morning.

Bernard had breakfasted and left the farmhouse in full view of his parents.

"We're going on a long bike ride." He told them as he packed up bread and cheese and bottles of tea into an already full satchel.

"In the middle of December?" his mother queried.

"It's going to be a bright and crisp day", his father nodded. "Enjoy it, son."

Bernard wondered if his father suspected his plan; but he thought it best not to ask.

Barbara had not had anyone to talk to, as her parents didn't formally rise until half past seven. She had dressed in the dark, washed in the kitchen and eaten apples for breakfast. She left a note in the middle of the kitchen table – 'Gone for a bike ride'. This didn't seem quite adequate. So she added later 'Heading for Scotland with friends, back in a few days.' Best that she did that, so they didn't bother the police with a search party. Barbara left a dark and cold house behind her as she wheeled her bike down the driveway.

"Got a map?" Barbara whispered as they hugged a greeting.

"Yes. Are you sure you want to do this? It's a good 60 miles."

Barbara nodded. He just saw the outline of her bobble hat waving. "Do you think we can manage it in one day?"

"No, I think we should stop over somewhere around Carlisle. We'll find a pub or something. I've got three pounds with me."

"Alright, let's get going then."

"Be careful. There's a heavy frost."

They set off towards the Carlisle road, the moon at their shoulders, not needing to speak. As the sky turned azure and the moon faded, they stopped to drink some cold tea and tighten their scarves. It was around the same time that Barbara's mother had found her note on the kitchen table. She gone downstairs to light the stove and make the tea while her husband prepared himself for work. He came downstairs a little later to find the kettle singing and his wife in a daze. He treated her gently. They used to have a domestic to do this sort of thing before the war. Even now that war was over, domestics were impossible to find, so she had ruined her hands doing it all herself. "Everything alright, dear?" He held back with an offer of help until he knew what the trouble was.

"I'm not sure. Look at this…" she handed the note over.

He adjusted his spectacles. "Gone for a bike ride to Scotland?"

"Setting off in the dark without warning us."

"Yes."

"Dear, do you think she might have gone to Gretna Green with that farmer chap?"

"What makes you think that?"

"I was her age once. And I see more than she realises."

They looked at one another in silent agreement that this could well be the case.

"What are we to do?" Barbara's mother began to twist the rope on her dressing gown.

"Hurry with the breakfast and I'll call at that chap's farm on my way to the office. See if he's missing as well."

Of course the farmer chap was also on a bike ride to Scotland, and his father had a suspicious twinkle in his eye as he told Barbara's father so. This tipped the usually affable solicitor into something resembling a rage. He at once determined to go after them in his car, and hang the petrol ration. He told Bernard's father of his suspicions and of his intention, then asked him what route he thought they might have taken.

"Well, I don't rightly know." Bernard's father drawled slowly and rubbed his chin. "I could get the map out and we could have a look."

"Yes. Please do that."

"Ah! But he'll have taken it with him, won't he?"

"We have to stop them. Are you going to come with me?"

"Me?" The farmer shook his head. "Too much to do here, and I'm a pair of hands short. The chickens won't count themselves."

"I see. Well, I shall go after them myself."

Pausing at a telephone box first, to explain the situation to his wife and to instruct her to telephone his office, Barbara's father took to the road. He was held up by other vehicles moving slowly. Although the sun had now risen, the hills still sparkled white. The wiser, more untroubled drivers know that those sections of road in shadow might be a rink of black ice. This preoccupied driver, however, overtook and for the first time in his life, he exceeded the speed limit. He sped through two small towns, almost killing a dog en route until; at last, he spotted two cyclists breasting a hill in the distance. He squeezed the accelerator, realised the perilous position of petrol and eased off again quickly. He had them in his sight now. He edged up behind them and hooted the car horn. Barbara, at the rear, turned around and saw her family car.

"Bernard! It's my father!" she called. The wind was flowing downwards; Bernard barely heard what she said. He looked over his shoulder and wobbled a little.

"What?"

"My father!"

He saw the car and finally realised the situation.

"Don't stop! Keep going!"

They powered ahead as the road began to drop into a valley. Barbara's father hooted his horn again and began to wrestle with the side window, finally opening it and calling to her. "Barbara! Stop at once!" The car swerved a little, he pulled his head back in and concentrated on the driving. The road dipped and then began a curving climb. The cyclists' speed dropped and the car began to gain on them again. The horn went off again and this time Barbara's father attempted to overtake. There was a drop to the left, he thought that he might be able to hem them in and block their passage forward. Barbara began to tire and she fell back a little, but Bernard powered on – head down and calves throbbing. Whether it was black ice caused by the shade of a crag or the sudden appearance of a van bearing down on him, Barbara's father was never sure. Perhaps it was a little of both. But the end result was Bernard cartwheeling over the grass verge; rolling down the embankment and landing face down with his bike across his legs. Barbara screamed. The driver of the van stopped jumped from behind the wheel.

"I saw it all, Miss! It was all his fault!"

The van driver pointed at her father, who remained in his stalled car staring blankly ahead.

A Provincial Arrival

By the time that Sheila reached her home station it was past supper time. She had changed trains in Sheffield, eaten a flabby meat pie and reacquainted herself with the air of the industrial north. Even in the waiting room, she could hear the familiar boom of the steelworks in the valley beyond. What a change from tropical insects. It was all enough to make her want her own bed, even though she had not slept in it for two years.

Home was a five minute walk from the station. The engine and two carriages of the local stopping train chugged off leisurely as she crossed the peeling lattice footbridge. The next stop was only three miles away; it was hardly worth getting any speed up. Sheila walked down two terraced streets and then began the hill climb. Terraces made way for semis. There was her home, at last, at the head of a cul-de-sac. A light shone from the mock-Tudor canopied side door. This led immediately into the kitchen – she made her entrance, announcing magnificently that she was back, dropping her baggage on the lino with a thump.

A small shriek answered her, and a knife clattered to the floor. A tiny, brightly dyed woman stood in the corner of the kitchen, spreading slices of grey bread with a thimble sized piece of butter.
"Oh! Hello. It's Mrs Parkin isn't it?"

With a sudden flush, Sheila thought that she must have got the wrong house. She had been away a long time after all. But no, that wasn't the case. The furniture was the same. Although some of the pictures on the walls were different. The tiny woman wiped her hands on her frilly apron and tottered over to Sheila. She touched her arm.

"Hello dearie, your father's in the lounge listening to the radio. Go and have a few words with him. I'll make myself scarce for a while, and then I'll bring you some tea in."

Sheila, too bemused to argue, went into the room that she presumed was meant by 'the lounge'. Raucous band music played on his radio set and her father stood and switched it off as she walked into the room.

"Hello, love! We'd all but given up on you!"

"Hello Dad. Sorry. You know how it is; it took ages to get off the boat. Then I missed a train and had to wait ages in Sheffield for the local. Where's Mum?"

The fact that her mother was absent pressed on her quite suddenly. Things were missing in the room that denoted her presence…a cushion, a photograph, her knitting bag. Sheila had looked for them while she spoke.

"Sit down love and I'll explain. She's alright, don't worry! We didn't tell you by letter because it didn't seem right. Your mother couldn't bear to cause you grief when she couldn't be there to comfort you. So we carried on as normal letter-writing wise. We… Well, your mother, she was always the letter writer…just didn't mention certain things. I think that she found it heavy going but there, it worked."

"What are you getting around to, Dad?" Sheila began to see, but all the same she wanted his explanation.

"Your mother and I got divorced about a year ago now. I stayed here and married again. Mrs Parkin as was – did you meet on the way in?" Sheila nodded

"Your mother went to live with your Aunt Dolly at her pub up in Leeds. Did you know that Uncle Fred had passed away?"

"Yes, Mum wrote to me about that."

Her father leaned over and patted her on the knee.

"We're all still friends. Your mother came down this

afternoon to wait for you, but went back home when you hadn't arrived by six o'clock. She's coming back again tomorrow, you'll see her then."

"I don't see. If you're still friends, why did you have to divorce? What happened?" Sheila stood and moved over to the mantelpiece, letting the fire burn into her cold legs.

"A lot happened. You know I was a warden for a while? We had a few raids. They aimed for the steelworks and missed. I had to go and help clear up the mess. I saw things and it made me change my way of thinking. I wanted to see a bit more of life, get out more, do more. Your Mum couldn't get on with me when I was being like that."

"I see. And this getting out a bit more involved seeing more of Mrs Parkin?"

"No, now don't you blame her. It was nothing to do with her. At first."

"So why?"

"Your mother got fed up. She said I was going to be the death of her. We had terrible arguments about things like my wanting to listen to the radio all the time. Then Uncle Fred got ill so she decided to go and help Dolly with the pub and everything. When he died she decided to stop there. She looks after things in the back room while Dolly does the bar work. She said she was happier there. So that's when I started courting Doris. We got married a few months ago."

"Married? Doris?"

"Mrs Parkin as was, yes."

"She's my stepmother?"

"Yes."

"Is there anything else you want to drop on me from a great height?"

"No, I think that's all. We'd better have some tea, eh?" He opened the door and called out to Doris to bring tea. Sheila sat down and stared into the fire.

"Get a bit closer, love. I bet you're feeling the cold. You look like you've seen a lot of sun. Tell us some of your adventures then."

"Well, I think I told you everything in my letters. Unlike you and Mum."

The door flung open with a light kick from Doris' trim little heeled shoe. She edged in, the large tea tray trimmed with burgundy roses rattling in her white knuckled hands. She placed it on the low table by the fireplace and began to pour tea into yellow china cups. The sight of the Sunday tea set from her childhood moved Sheila to tears.

"Oh here ducky, drink this. I'll make myself scarce again while you and your father carry on chatting."

"No, stay and drink your tea." Sheila sniffed.

Doris looked over at her husband – he nodded and she sat, demurely, her knees to one side.

"So what now? Is this still my home or am I just visiting?"

"Of course!" her father and step mother spoke at once.

"Your bedroom is just as you left it. It will always be yours. We won't be having any children will we dear?" Doris reddened at her own gaucherie. "My son will have the box room, when he eventually gets out of the navy."

"Oh. Of course. You've got two sons haven't you? Wasn't one in the year below me at school…?"

"I did have two boys, yes. Jimmy was in the RAF, That'll be him that you remember. He was shot down in 1941 I'm afraid."

Sheila half looked at her step mother, then drained her tea and poured another cup.

"But my Sam's still with us." Doris continued. "He's just waiting for his papers and he'll need somewhere to stay while he sorts himself out. Can't see him stopping long though. Bit of a wanderer. He once ran away to Huddersfield to see a trolley bus."

Sheila's father cleared his throat. "Your Mum and I spoke about this though. And there is room for you at Auntie Dolly's pub. They thought you might like to do a bit of entertaining for them, keep your hand in. Perhaps get spotted! There's a few theatres and the like up there too. It's up to you where you put down your new roots. But we'll always be glad to see you, won't we, Doris?"

"That's right."

They both looked at Sheila, waiting for a response. She put another spoonful of sugar in her tea and stirred.

"Well, spoiled for choice aren't I? I expect I'll go to Leeds with Mum tomorrow and have a look. What a welcome home I must say."

She took a packet of cigarettes from her bag and sighed loudly.

Heading for the Boat Train

Edie, her Mum and her baby found a compartment with spare seats and settled into them.

"Ere, can you make room for another?"

A young woman nursing a baby not much older than Edie's slid the door and poked her head in. Her grey-looking mother staggered sideways behind her as the train heaved away from Norwich station. Edie and her mother shuffled along and moved things from the spare seat next to them. The two new women squeezed in, passing the baby between them. As Edie and her mother continued their chat, it became obvious that she was heading for a sea voyage. The younger woman turned to Edie and smiled broadly

"You off to America as well?"

Edie felt her sharp elbow in her less than fleshy middle. "That's right. Expect we'll meet again when we get on the boat."

"Where's your husband live? My name's Pam by the way…"

"Edie. He lives in New York City."

"Oh I'm heading for New Jersey myself. Is it near to New York, do you know?"

"Erm, I'm not really sure. I've seen a map but I can't get the distances. My Robert says everything's much further apart than it looks."

"Oh I do hope she'll be near somebody what's English, don't you?" Pam's mother leaned across the two young women and spoke to her counterpart at the other end of the compartment. "Don't like to think of her being totally surrounded by foreigners."

"I keep telling you, Ma. John's Grandpa's English." Pam rolled her eyes and winked at Edie.

The train pulled along through the monochrome flat lands towards London. The women chatted, changed nappies balanced on their knees, fed, comforted and winded. The outskirts of the capital began to close in on the tracks. The women noticed bomb sites dominating and dropped their voices at the evidence that others had suffered more than they. The bombers too-ing and fro-ing to the bases had been one thing, but this must have been something else.

"We have to get to Waterloo." Edie turned to Pam.

"How were you thinking of getting there?"

"We thought we'd have a go at the underground, didn't we, Mum?"

"I've never been on the underground. It scares me a bit so we wondered about taking the bus."

"Well we haven't been to London ever at all. But our neighbour has, and he said that you're best on the underground trains and he gave us this map."

They looked at a hand drawn map that traced a route from Liverpool Strcct to Waterloo, with intermediate stations marked on and the blue dotted river. Station frontages were drawn at each end, just in case they ended up outside it and wanted to know what it looked like.

"Ooh but do we have to go under the river?" Edie's mother leaned in and pointed. "I don't fancy that at all. All that water on top of my head."

"Well, it's not fallen in yet, Mum." Edie pointed out. "I want to try it. I might not ever get another chance."

The compartment fell silent.

By the time that the small party reached Waterloo, Edie's mother made a direct aim for a bench, never minding the groups of women and children crossing her path. She flopped down onto it, took her felt hat off and began to fan her face with it.

"Your mother looks peaky" Pam's mother nudged her. "I don't like the look of her at all."

Edie looked over at the bench. It was being occupied not by her mother, but by a frail old grandmother.

"Mum? Are you feeling alright?"

"Mm. A bit hot. I'll come round in a mo."

"Hot? It must be near freezing in here. She's not right, dear."

The Boat Train was announced over the tannoy. Information boards clattered and lines of excited women converged on the platform gate.

"We need to be moving again, Mum, come on."

Edie's mother went to stand up, and then concertinaed to the concourse in a deft move that left her lying on her back. A crowd soon gathered around her. A porter held her hand, tapped her on the face and then went to fetch medical help. Edie's baby began to cry and Edie joined him. She turned to Pam and sent her on her way. "There's no sense in you missing the boat too. Mum! Stop it! Get up!"

Pam looked grim, and nodded. "I hope it all works out alright. Write to me…" She called out an address that was lost in the thrum of the station.

Later on, in the hospital, a young nurse took Edie's baby from her tired arms and showed her into a small room. A doctor waited for her there, bushy eyebrows meeting as he frowned over a piece of paper. He looked up only briefly when she entered, not smiling, unemotional. He instructed her to sit, and then kept

her waiting in silence for an aching two minutes.
Finally he told her that her mother was dying. She
had a few months to live. He was surprised that Edie
had no inkling, that the symptoms had not been
noticed over the past year. But then, yes, perhaps
she had deliberately hidden it, so as not to put her
daughter off from leaving. Shame, all these
daughters going after Yankee men with no thought to
their duties at home.

"I'll stay here until the end." Edie told him. I won't go
until she does."

Epilogue

The man who went under the Cornish Express just
outside Plymouth station was identified as Peter Bell.
His wife, who was a resident of a genteel suburb of
the town, was promptly informed. She buried him at a
sparsely attended funeral, sold the semi- detached
villa and went to live with her parents in Bristol.

On the other side of the Tamar, another wife became increasingly worried that her husband had disappeared. He was always away for fairly lengthy periods, so she did not mention it to the police until spring was well advanced. The police contacted the army, who told them that the person they sought, Herbert Minton, had been killed in action in 1942. A newspaper appeal helped to solve Mrs Minton's mystery. She cried for six weeks solid, then married a policeman.

***

Catherine chose to divorce Henry and marry Bill Tanner. He sold his garage and opened another forty miles away, near the coast. Catherine gave birth to a baby girl on her honeymoon. She and Bill doted on their daughter and had a happy marriage. However, Catherine gained a daughter but lost two sons. As she had anticipated, Henry demanded custody and set about a campaign of disgust at his sons' mother's actions. She was not allowed to see them. She tried to contact them when they came of age but they did not respond. Her youngest son, after going through a divorce himself, did make his peace with Catherine just before her death in 1980. But she never saw her eldest son again.

***

Arthur realised that betting on the dogs was never going to make him rich. So he turned to the football pools instead. He successfully built up a life of escapism round the scores and the league tables. He drove Mary crackers with his charts, notebooks and coupons which had to be carefully cleared off the table before every meal. He won £100 on one occasion.

Bob was unable to walk away from his addiction and he led a peripatetic life after being discharged from the navy. In the end he became a bookmaker and found himself considerably better off.

***

Bernard was very lucky. He survived the tumble from his bike with just a couple of broken bones and some nasty grazing. He told Barbara's father that he would ask the police not to charge him and tell them that the accident was mostly his own fault. Of course there was a condition to his kindness. He and Barbara were married with her father's consent later the following spring. Barbara made an excellent farmer and her marriage was fertile and fruitful too – to her parents' reluctant admiration. The fateful bike ride to Gretna Green became a family legend, and is still spoken of in several County Durham households today.

***

Sheila moved to Leeds and got herself an acting position in the local rep theatre as well as doing a bit of singing in her Aunt's pub. After a year or two she tired of the provincial life and went to London. She found a bit of supporting work on the stage and radio but never became a household name. After one dismal audition, she overheard two men discussing 'all these ENSA types, thinking that their war work entitles them to theatrical stardom, when half of them have no talent.' Sheila took the remark personally and went to stay with her Father and Doris while she licked her searing wound. There she met Sam Parkin, who was ensconced in the box room and working as a driver. She decided that she could do worse and married him.

***

Edie got her Mum home and took over the running of their household. Her failure to arrive in New York caused quite a bother and a heated exchange of letters took place between the estranged spouses. Robert was angry at the waste of a good ticket – and at having to hire extra help for the store. As soon as he had saved enough, he would come over to Norfolk and fetch her himself. So he said.

However, the local newly-qualified doctor took a shine to Edie when he first visited her mother. He began to call regularly (at no extra charge) and insisted on taking her out for some respite. In the end, the nearest she ever got to New York was Newquay – where she went on honeymoon with the doctor when the transatlantic divorce was finally resolved.

Enjoy this book?
Why not read The History Usherette's
Second Seat, Third Row?
Find out about a South London audience
for 'A Canterbury Tale', August 1944.

Printed in Great Britain
by Amazon